Josie

the Singing Butterfly

Volume 2 / Adventures #6-10

Josie Waverly

Illustrations by: Frances Espanol

Print information available on the last page

Rev. date: 01/28/2016

To order additional copies of this book, contact:
Xlibris
1-888-795-4274
www.Xlibris.com
Orders@Xlibris.com

Adventure #6

"JOSIE BATTLES THE BEES"

Bobby Bee was being bullied
by the bad bees in the bunch.
Josie, the singing butterfly,
flew down to help Bobby Bee.
She was following a hunch!

As she flew closer she saw
they were all bullying him.
She yelled "Hey you bad bees,
stop bullying my good friend!"
But the bad bees just kept bullying Bobby Bee
Again, again, and again!

Josie began to sing a song,
really loud and with all her might!
A song about how bullying and
how being mean to others is
JUST NOT RIGHT!
She sang about how mean words can break a heart
and how bad they can make someone feel.
She sang about how pushing and shoving can cause
a hurt that will take a long time to heal!

5

The bees in the bunch began to listen.
They no longer wanted to be bad.
Josie said, "Please be nice to
my friend Bobby Bee."
All the bees said they would
and this made Josie glad!

Josie's Lesson:
No one likes to be bullied!
Stand up for others.

Adventure #7

"JOSIE & CHARLIE CHIPMUNK"

"Oh my gosh" said Charlie Chipmunk,
"I can't get in my hole!"
"But I see Mr. Mouse can, and so can Mr. Mole."
He said, "I must have eaten too much today.
All my nuts have gone away."
Sad, he sat there alone on the ground.
Josie the singing butterfly heard what he said
and she came fluttering down.

9

Josie said, "Hey Charlie Chipmunk
maybe I can help you!
Follow me now for a run or two.
Chase me until I say to stop.
From the bottom of this tree
and then right up to the top!"

Josie fluttered over and said,
"It's ok Charlie Chipmunk,
now try your hole again."
He smiled, thanked Josie for her help,
then he slipped right in!

Josie's Lesson:
For a long life,
exercise and eat right!

Adventure #8

"JOSIE SEES DOLLY'S BEAUTY"

Five little ducklings waddling in a row.
With number six lagging behind in tow.
Josie the singing butterfly flew down to see...
Why is number six so far behind?
What could the problem possibly be?

Josie asked Dolly Duck "Why are you so slow?"
Dolly said sadly, "I'm not slow!
They just don't want me to go.
They all have pretty long feathers that are yellow, soft, and fluffy.
Mine are short and brown, and my bill's a little puffy."

"They think because I look different
that I'm not one of them!"
Josie said, "Oh Dolly Duck, you are a special gem!
You look different this is true
and they look alike no doubt.
But anyone can look the same,
your look makes you stand out!"

17

"So shine your light as bright as you can,
Dolly Duck.
Hold your head up to the sky.
With your special and unique features
you'll be flying high!"
Then Josie and Dolly Duck sang together as they followed all the rest.
Dolly said, "Thanks for the kind words Josie,
as a friend, you are the best!

18

Josie's Lesson:
Being different is okay!
You are special! Everyone is!

Adventure #9

"JOSIE MEETS MYA MOUSE"

Mya Mouse was walking home from school
with her book bag right beside her.
When she came upon Josie the singing
butterfly sitting on a flower.
Josie said, "Hi Mya Mouse how was school today?"
"My first day was not so good," said Mya Mouse,
"No one wanted to play."

21

She said, "The other mice are bigger than me
so they all left me out."
"Well you need to get their attention" said Josie.
"Though, that doesn't mean you have to
scream and shout."

22

"I will teach you a song to sing,
that you can share with all."
So Josie sang, then Mya Mouse sang,
they just had a balll

23

Mya Mouse went to school the next day,
with her new song in her head.
Josie flew down to the window sill
and watched as Mya lead.
She was singing and teaching
them her new favorite song.
Before she knew it they were all singing along.
Everyone then asked Mya Mouse to play,
and she had a much better second day!

Josie's Lesson:
You are never too little to make
a BIG difference!

Adventure #10

"JOSIE LEADS LILY LAMB"

Lily Lamb was singing and dancing
around the meadow so silly.
When her momma said
"Come on now my little silly Lily."
But Lily Lamb didn't listen
and just kept on doing her thing.
When Josie, the singing butterfly flew in,
they both started to sing.

All of a sudden Lily Lamb stopped singing
and took a look around.
But her momma was not there
and was nowhere to be found.
Josie asked, "What's wrong Lily?
You were dancing so merrily."
Lily Lamb said, "I know but now
I think my momma has left me."

"Left you?" questioned Josie,
"Did she tell you to come along?"
"Yes!" said Lily Lamb,
"but I was too busy singing my song."
Lily said, "I'm scared now Josie.
Will I ever find my momma again?"
Josie said, "Don't you worry
Lily Lamb. We will find her.
Follow me my friend."

Josie flew up and flew down,
then around and around.
Soon she spotted momma sheep
right there on the ground.
"Lily Lamb she's right there!, Josie shouted,
"Run to the big oak tree!"
Then they both sang with joy, together again,
happy as can be.

30

Josie's Lesson:

Always listen!
Be aware of your surroundings.

Printed in the United States
By Bookmasters